Kidnapped to the Center of the Earth

The Troll Family Adventures™

Book One

Kidnapped to the Center
of the Earth

By FamilyVision Press

FamilyVision Press
New York

Kidnapped To The Center of the Earth

FamilyVision Press™
For The Family That Reads Together™
An imprint of Multi Media Communicators, Inc.
575 Madison Avenue, Suite 1006
New York, NY 10022

FamilyVision Press™, Troll Family Adventures™ and For The Family That Reads Together™ are trademarks of Multi Media Communicators, Inc.

Created by Thomas L. Tedrow

Managing Editor, Maggie Holmes

Cover and interior art by Michael A. Hernandez, Jr.

Typesetter, Samuel Chapin

Library of Congress Catalog Card Number: 93-071554

ISBN 1-56969-125-8

10 9 8 7 6 5 4 3 2 1
First Edition

Printed in the United States of America

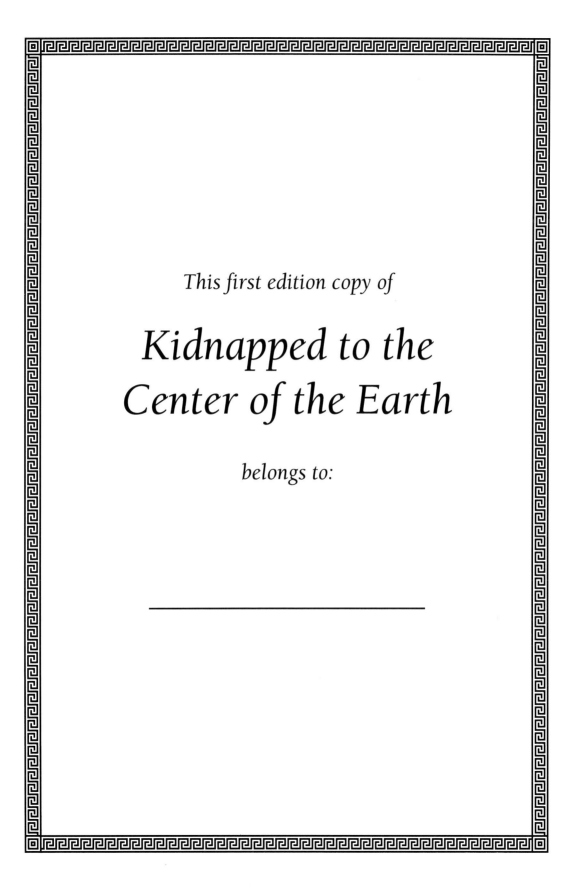

This first edition copy of

Kidnapped to the Center of the Earth

belongs to:

_____

A Message to Parents and Guardians
from FamilyVision Press

At FamilyVision, we believe that families should read together. Whether your children set aside a specially reserved family reading time or whether they read books, newspapers, trading cards, or cereal boxes at the breakfast table, please urge your children to read, read, read!

So where do you start? At your children's earliest age and throughout their lifetime, read and discuss books aloud during regularly scheduled reading times. Make reading time a special time—take turns reading, encourage discussion and questions, have grandparents relate personal stories from their childhood, ask your child to retell parts of the story and anticipate what will happen next.

Let them hear the music and power of the written word spoken aloud. Enhance the storytelling moment by varying facial expressions, tone, and pace as you read. Give the reluctant reader flexibility to move around or use crayons and pencils while the story is being read. And, for younger children, add another dimension to reading with a "read and play" experience. For example, when reading our Troll Family Adventures, let your child hold a toy troll. When reading is completed, help your child play out the storyline or create new adventures.

Where can you get your books? Make the local bookstore and library part of your family's regular routine. Take them to the library's storytime and watch for such special events as readings and personal appearances at bookstores. Remember to take a book everywhere! It's amazing when and where there will be time to read.

When you read with your children, they will learn firsthand that a book can be a wonderful thing. It can be a vehicle for traveling to new worlds, a key to unlocking the imagination, and a wonderful opportunity for sharing special moments with your children.

In our *Kidnapped to the Center of the Earth,* Tabby loses her wings. With reading, you can give your children wings that last a lifetime.

The Truth About Trolls

Legend has it that Trolls lived under bridges or in caves in Scandinavia. Some people made up stories about Trolls, saying they were guardians of buried treasure and the keepers of rainbows.

Since no one had ever seen Trolls, stories and myths developed that they came out only at night, loved to eat berries and could grant a wish if you rubbed their hair. Some people even wrote books that said Trolls were ugly, greedy, troublesome creatures who stole dogs!

But they were wrong!

These stories were all made up by people who didn't know anything about the *real* Trolls. Toys were created based upon these make-believe stories about naked trolls who ride skateboards and stick gemstones in their belly buttons.

It's time to let the truth be known. Trolls don't run around naked or do those other things. The little people of the forest exist, living somewhere between here and there, in harmony with nature. They are naturally peaceful beings with no prejudices, untouched by human contact.

Though the Trolls do not want to come forward to show the world where they really live, one Troll family has sent us a book called *The Troll Family Adventures*. They want the world to know the truth about who they really are and what Trolls are really like.

It's a very special book which we are proud to print. Each adventure is a book in itself, so look for all their wonderful stories in the future.

Contents

Who Are Trolls?

My name is Tom, but everyone calls me Pa Troll. My wife is Tammy. We have three youngsters, Trixie, Tabby and Toby.

We have all helped to write this book so that you humans will see we are not fat, pudgy dolls who have nothing better to do than stick rhinestones in our belly buttons and run around naked.

I don't know who started the silly stories about us, but when we found a troll doll in the woods that one of your human children had left behind, we knew that we had to write this book.

Who are we? We are Trolls. Trolls are very much like other earthdwellers, except that we always get along with each other.

We don't make war, and we treat everyone as equals, and we live in peace and harmony. That's why Trolls are so happy.

We have hair the colors of the rainbow, which is why many humans think that we are rainbow keepers and masters of the beautiful bands of color that nature shares with us after a rain shower.

But we, like you, admire rainbows because they remind us that we are all part of nature's plan. We live in harmony with nature and all its natural resources.

Trolls have pets, just like you humans do. We have TrollCats, TrollDogs and TrollBirds.

We don't like Trats—Troll Rats—and are afraid of MoleTrolls, but I'll tell you more about them later.

When a Troll is born, a magical birthstone is laid on his or her chest. As it begins to glow, it shows what color hair the Troll baby will have.

Each Troll keeps his or her birthstone for the rest of his or her life. Worn on a necklace, the birthstone always reflects the emotions of the Troll wearing it. That is why Trolls naturally tell the truth.

When a Troll gets married, the most important part of the ceremony is when the birthstones are moved from the necklaces and put into rings which are worn as a symbol of commitment to each other.

Trolls are born with small wings which we shed during our fourth year of life. We mount the wings over our beds when we are young, to remind us that life is full of changes.

But until we shed our wings, it is hard for parents to keep up with their little flying Trolls. So Troll mothers have to keep their baby Trolls tied to the ground, or to their wrists like humans do with balloons.

Trolls can also jump very high, which allows us to have fun, escape from danger and jump up to the tree houses where we make our homes.

Meet the Troll Family

As I said, most everyone calls me Pa Troll and I'm a Troll historian, so that's why I know so much about our people. I hope one day to write a book about such famous Trolls in history as Davy Trollkett and Robin Troll and his band of merry Trolls.

Tammy, my wife, works for a Trollvironmental Group that keeps our forests clean. When we can find a baby TrollSitter, we love to go out jump dancing and eat Itrollian food. We have three little Trolls.

Trixie is ten years old and has flaming red hair. She likes Rock and Troll music and to do the latest jump dances on TTV (Troll TV).

Toby is eight, has long blue hair and is always into good-natured mischief. He loves to run and jump and hates to do yard work under the tree house.

Tabby is four, has blond hair, and hasn't lost her wings yet. She manages to turn almost everything she touches into a troubling mess and is always wandering away.

We've taken the time to write down things that have happened to our Troll family, and want to share some of our adventures with you.

Tales of MoleTrolls

$\mathbb{T}$ rolls make their homes in trees because long ago we feared the MoleTrolls, evil creatures who used to come up from a hole in the ground at night to steal Troll children. MoleTrolls love baby Trolls hair and would cut it off to make special robes.

Although I have never seen a MoleTroll, I have heard the tales that are passed down and the scary stories that are told at night to keep the young Trolls from sneaking out after dark.

No one I know has ever seen a MoleTroll because a hundred years ago, the elder Trolls got together and made a heavy metal

cover. They put it over the MoleTroll hole in the ground, which leads to the center of the earth. A torch burns beside it to remind Trolls of the danger below.

The MoleTrolls have tried to push the cover off, but they are not strong enough. Sometimes, when the evening wind is calm, you can stand by the cover and hear what sounds like the MoleTrolls scratching to get out.

Young Trolls are taken to the metal cover and told that waiting just below the surface are the horrible, green MoleTrolls who would reach up and grab them if the cover was ever removed.

We live near the hole, so I always made sure that each of my three Troll children were told about the terrible MoleTrolls. A couple of times I caught Toby and Trixie Troll running and jumping over the cover, but I knew they would never to try to move it.

Then the warquakes started happening more frequently. They began when humans were at war. Warquakes, like earthquakes, cause the ground to shake violently. We Trolls had to adjust our peaceful lives to that of an unpeaceful human world.

We developed safety rules. But one warquake was more intense than any others. Our houses shook. Trees began falling. And the ground cracked open.

This is the story that my Troll children told me about the day the ground cracked.

The Day the Ground Cracked

Trixie and Toby were playing jump-jump over the metal cover. They were supposed to be watching Tabby, but instead they'd tied her string to the metal cover so they could play games.

"I hope her string doesn't break," Toby said, pulling a leaf from his blue hair.

"It won't," Trixie smiled. "And I tied a double knot so she won't get loose."

"But you put on the extra long string ball," Toby said, worried that Tabby might float too high.

"I hooked most of it around her belt. She will never get higher than we can jump," Trixie replied.

"Let's play jump-and-double-jump," Toby said.

"But our birthstones might fall off," Trixie worried, knowing that jump-and-double-jump was a rough-and-tumble game.

"Then let's hang them on that tree," Toby said pointing.

They hung their birthstones on a branch and played jump-and-double-jump around the cover that sealed off the MoleTroll tunnels.

Suddenly the ground shook from a warquake. Toby fell to the ground and was very scared.

From across the way, Trixie jumped up in the air and landed by Toby. "Just hold onto my arm," she said, pushing her red hair from her eyes.

"But look at that," Toby said, pointing to a crack in the ground. The warquake had moved the cover to the MoleTroll hole!

"Where's Tabby?" he asked.

Trixie looked around. "I don't see her."

Suddenly they saw her. Tabby was flying high above the uncovered hole. She had untied the knot that held her and was floating in the air, holding the string in her hands. Her birthstone was glowing in bright rainbow colors, indicating she was having fun.

"Come down here! Hurry! We're in danger!" Trixie shouted.

"No!" said Tabby, doing a loop-the-loop in the air. She flew just above their heads, shaking her shaggy blond hair.

"I hope her wings fall off right now," Toby grumbled. He knew that Tabby's wings were about to come off, since she was four years old.

Then the ground shook again and a falling tree branch knocked Tabby to the ground. "I want Ma," she cried, rubbing her head.

Toby tried to stand, but the shaking earth was like a boat on the ocean. When the earth stopped moving, Toby saw a terrible face staring at him.

"Look!" he said, pointing towards the hole.

"Oh my gosh," said Trixie.

Looking out of the hole was a MoleTroll! It was green, had beady red eyes and was wearing a moldy green robe. The creature was just as the stories described. Then it was gone.

"Did you see that?" Toby asked. Trixie nodded.

Tabby crawled to the hole and looked down. "I see you," she giggled, pointing her finger.

"Get away!" Toby called out.

But when nothing happened, curiosity got the best of them. Trixie and Toby slowly walked over to the hole and looked down.

"I guess he's gone," Trixie said. "We better go home and warn Pa and the others that the warquake has knocked off the MoleTroll cover."

"Yeah," said Toby, turning to go. But they forgot to grab Tabby's string. She began floating upward, flapping her little wings.

"Get her," Toby said.

They jumped up to grab her but Tabby was too quick. "Can't catch me," she giggled.

"You're going to be in trouble if you don't come down here right now," Trixie said.

Then Tabby started to come down as if someone was pulling on her string.

Tabby was laughing until she saw it was the MoleTroll who was pulling her. He had the string and was reeling her down into the hole.

Toby tried to grab Tabby but he missed. "Help!" she cried, as she was pulled into the hole in the ground.

The glow of Tabby's birthstone dimmed in fear. Then she was gone.

Kidnapped to the Center of the Earth

Trixie leaned over the edge, trying to see where Tabby had gone. "I can't see her," she cried.

Toby looked down, but it was too dark. "Let's get Pa."

Then they heard Tabby cry out. "Help me!"

Toby grabbed the torch and stuck it into the hole. "There she is!" Trixie cried, pointing down into the tunnel.

"Toby, Trixie, help me!" Tabby screamed. The MoleTroll was carrying her down the tunnel towards the center of the earth.

"What shall we do?" Toby asked.

Trixie took a deep breath. "We've got to save her!" she said, jumping down into the hole.

"But we should get Pa," Toby said.

"If we get Pa we'll lose sight of Tabby," Trixie said. "There's no time. Come on, follow me."

They raced down the tunnel trying to catch up to the mean, ugly MoleTroll. "Let my sister go!" Trixie shouted. The MoleTroll just grunted *"no."*

Tabby struggled to get free, but the MoleTroll gripped her tightly. As he ran, the ugly creature looked at her blond hair.

"Your yellow hair will make a nice robe," he grunted.

"I want my Ma," Tabby cried, but the MoleTroll ignored her.

The MoleTroll looked back and saw the light of the torch and knew he was being followed.

"Stop!" Toby's voice echoed through the tunnel.

"I'll never undo my string again," Tabby moaned to herself. Then she came up with an idea!

Worried that Trixie and Toby would not be able to keep up with the MoleTroll, she began unraveling her string. "Please see it," she whispered, leaving a trail of string behind.

Tabby had done it just in time, because the MoleTroll turned down another tunnel and began weaving through an underground maze to throw the Troll children off his track. "They'll never find you now," he laughed.

*   *   *

Trixie came to the fork in the tunnel. "Which way did they go?" she asked.

Toby looked around. "I don't see anything."

Then Trixie saw the string. "Look," she said, picking up the loose end. "It's Tabby's string. She left us a trail."

"Let's follow it!" Toby shouted.

Trixie collected the string as they ran through the maze of tunnels. "How much string was on the ball?" Toby called out, ducking to avoid a low-hanging rock.

"Pa said that there was enough string on her line to float up to the clouds," she said.

"Let's hope so and let's hope the string doesn't break," Toby worried, shaking his head in the torchlight.

The MoleTroll Cavern

The MoleTroll didn't know that Tabby was leaving a trail of string behind for Trixie and Toby to follow. He was so confident that he'd lost them, that he ran straight into the main MoleTroll cavern near the center of the earth.

"MoleTrolls, come look!" he shouted.

It had been over a hundred years since a Troll had been kidnapped and brought underground. They hadn't made a Troll-hair robe since before that MoleTroll's grandfather was born.

"I have a Troll!" he shouted out. "We have new Troll hair!"

MoleTrolls came out from small caves around the cavern that glowed with the light of strange, blue stones that lined the walls. Its eerie glow cast the room in unearthly shadows.

"Troll hair, Troll hair!" the MoleTrolls grunted. They all wanted to see and touch Tabby's hair.

"Leave me alone!" she shouted, but the MoleTrolls wouldn't listen.

"We have Troll hair!" they laughed, hugging each other.

It was a special occasion for the MoleTrolls. The MoleTrolls began dancing in circles. They were getting ready to cut Tabby's hair!

*   *   *

Up on the surface, Pa and Tammy Troll went looking for their children. They found the crack in the earth and the open MoleTroll hole.

"Where are the children?" Tammy asked.

Pa Troll looked around. "I guess they ran off when the quakes started." He looked at the hole. "I'm just glad they weren't anywhere near here," he said, running back toward the center of the forest.

"Where are you going?" Tammy called out.

"I have to tell everyone that the cover's been moved. We need to push it back before any MoleTrolls come out."

Tammy Troll looked at the dark hole, feeling that something wasn't right.

"I wonder what happened to the torch," she thought. Goose bumps went up her arms as she looked down into the hole.

Wings

Meanwhile Toby and Trixie heard the noise from the MoleTroll's cavern, so they left the torch in the tunnel and crept forward.

"You've got to have MoleTroll eyes to see in the dark," Toby grumbled.

"There's some kind of light up ahead," Trixie whispered.

"I say we go back and get the torch," he said.

Trixie held her finger to her lips. "Be quiet," she whispered, pointing to the dancing MoleTrolls.

"There's Tabby," he said. "That MoleTroll's holding her tight."

"This is bad news," Trixie said. She'd heard all the terrible stories about the MoleTrolls and didn't want to scare her brother.

"What are they doing?" Toby asked.

Trixie saw the MoleTrolls touching Tabby's hair. "I think they're going to cut off her hair."

"We've got to stop them," Toby whispered. Then he counted the MoleTrolls. There were more than he had fingers and toes.

"What are we going to do?" he asked.

"Let me think of something," Trixie said. Then she remembered the string in her hand.

"What are you doing?" Toby asked.

"I hope this string doesn't break," Trixie said. She was pulling on the string that was still attached to Tabby.

Tabby felt the tug on the string and looked around. She smiled when she saw her brother and sister hidden in the corner of the cavern. Her birthstone began to glow with excitement.

Trixie mouthed the words, jump-jump, to Tabby, hoping she would understand. Tabby nodded that she did.

The MoleTrolls brought out a pair of golden scissors to cut Tabby's hair and marched towards her. "Pull hard," Toby said.

Trixie yanked on the string and Tabby slipped out of the MoleTroll's arms. "Jump-jump!" Toby screamed.

Tabby shook her hair and when her feet touched the ground, she pushed off into the air. "Grab the Troll!" the MoleTrolls shouted.

"Pull her in," Toby said.

"I'm trying," Trixie said.

But Tabby was having the time of her life, flying to the top of the cavern and breaking off pieces of rock. Then she'd zoom down on the MoleTrolls and bop them on the head.

"Look at her birthstone," Toby grumbled. Her stone was flashing in rainbow colors because she was having so much fun.

"Oh, no. Not now!" Trixie exclaimed. One of Tabby's wings was coming loose!

"I told you it was going to happen soon," Toby said. "Pa never let me fly when I turned four."

Trixie reeled in the string as fast as she could. She was just in time.

When Tabby was five feet above their heads, her wings fell off and she dropped into Toby's arms. "That was fun," Tabby said.

"We better get out of here," Trixie said.

The MoleTrolls were running towards them shouting, "Trolls, Trolls, Trolls!" They now wanted to cut the hair off all three of the Troll children.

"Come on!" Trixie said.

"But what about my wings?" Tabby cried. She didn't want to be the only MoleTroll who didn't have her wings up on her wall.

"I'll grab 'em," Toby said, picking them up and putting them under his belt.

But by now the MoleTrolls had them surrounded. There was no way out.

"We're trapped," Trixie said, as the MoleTrolls closed in.

Toby touched his hair and looked around. "We *are* trapped!"

Tabby shook her head. "No we're not," she said, pointing up.

"What are you talking about?" Toby said.

Tabby pointed to the ledge around the cavern. "Play jump-jump and get to the ledge."

Trixie nodded. "It's our only hope."

The Trolls jumped as high as they could. Toby landed on the ledge first, followed by Trixie. But Tabby was smaller and had never jumped that high before.

"Help me," she cried, falling back towards the MoleTrolls who were reaching out from below, closing in on her.

Trixie still had the string in her hand and pulled Tabby to safety. "Thanks," she smiled, her birthstone throbbing in warm colors.

"We'd better run," Toby said. The MoleTrolls were putting up ladders to get to the ledge.

"This way!" Trixie said, leading the way to the same tunnel they'd come through—the one that led back to the surface—and away from the MoleTrolls.

Cover the Hole

Pa Troll had brought enough Trolls from the forest to push the cover back over the hole and seal it forever. "Let's do it quick," Pa said, worried that the creatures might get out.

Tammy Troll was still upset. She hadn't seen her three little Trolls yet and feared that something bad had happened to them.

Then she saw the two birthstones hanging on the tree. "Those belong to Toby and Trixie," she said, taking them off the branch.

Pa and the other Trolls had lifted the heavy cover and were preparing to set it back down over the hole. "Wait!" Tammy cried out.

"What is it?" Pa Troll asked.

"Toby and Trixie left their birthstones here," she said, "by the hole."

Pa and the other Trolls looked at the glowing stones in Tammy Troll's hands. They were glowing red and yellow.

"Our little Trolls are in danger. Look at the stones," Pa said, looking at the other Trolls.

"Let's cover the hole and go find them," one of the Trolls said. "Maybe they're lost in the forest somewhere."

"Good idea," Pa said, but Tammy put her hand on Pa's arm.

"I think they're down in the hole," she said, pointing to the MoleTroll tunnel that legend said led to the center of the earth.

* * *

Down in that dark hole, Trixie held onto Tabby's hand as they raced back up the tunnel toward the surface. "Hurry," she called out to Toby, who was lagging behind.

She didn't hear him answer so she stopped and held up the torch. "Where are you?"

"I'm coming," he panted, "but I twisted my ankle."

He wanted to stop and rest but he couldn't. The MoleTrolls were right behind them.

"Do you have my wings?" Tabby called out.

"They're under my belt," Toby said.

"There's daylight up ahead!" Trixie shouted. Tabby's birthstone began throbbing in excitement as they approached the hole.

Then the light started to disappear. "They're covering the hole!" Toby shouted.

* * *

Up above, Tammy Troll squeezed Pa's hand. "*Please* don't cover the hole. I can feel them down there."

A big Troll shook his head. "If your little Trolls are down there, then they're gone. I say we close off the hole before the MoleTrolls get out and other Trolls get lost."

Just then they heard Trixie's voice come up through the hole. "Wait! We're coming!"

"It's Trixie!" Tammy Troll said.

"It's us," Toby shouted, his voice echoing from the hole.

Pa looked at the other Trolls. "Move the cover back. My little Trolls are down there."

When they set the cover down away from the hole, the children heard familiar voices. "Are you okay?" Tammy Troll called out.

Trixie appeared at the bottom of the hole. "We're down here," she said, lifting her little sister up. "Take her," she said, unhooking the string from Tabby's belt.

"My baby," Tammy said, lifting Tabby up and hugging her.

41

"Jump out," Pa said, looking at Trixie.

But Toby's limp had caused him to fall behind. "I've got to help Toby," she said, handing up the torch and heading back to help him.

The MoleTrolls were closing in on Toby, but Trixie jumped between them. "Make your way to the hole," she said.

"What about you?" he asked, limping towards the light from the hole.

"I've got an idea," Trixie said.

"What?" Toby asked, worried about his sister.

"You jump up to safety. Just don't drop Tabby's wings."

"I won't," Toby said, "but you better hurry."

With the MoleTrolls almost upon her, Trixie looped the string around rocks on both sides of the tunnel.

"Troll hair, Troll hair," the MoleTrolls shouted, seeing Trixie and her long red hair almost within their grasp.

Tying the string tight, Trixie stuck her tongue out at the MoleTrolls. "Watch your step," she laughed, then ran back towards the hole.

"Jump up, Toby," Tammy shouted, seeing her little Troll below her.

"I can't. My ankle hurts," Toby moaned. He tried to jump on one leg but hardly got off the ground.

"Get on my shoulders," Trixie shouted as she ran up.

She picked him up and stood him on her shoulders. Just as they pulled Toby up to the surface, the MoleTrolls tripped on the string and fell into a squealing, squawking pile.

"Too bad, you clumsy creeps," Trixie laughed, then bent down and jumped up through the hole.

"Quick! Cover it up!" Pa shouted and the Trolls lifted the cover over the hole and dropped it back down in its place.

All was quiet for a moment, then the Trolls heard the scratching underneath. "The MoleTrolls are trying to get out," Toby gasped.

"They can't move the cover," Pa said, letting out a deep breath.

"But what if the earth cracks again?" Trixie asked.

Pa looked at the other Trolls and said, "Tomorrow, we will build a bigger cover to go over this one. We can never risk the MoleTrolls getting out."

Tammy Troll held out the birthstones to Trixie and Toby. "You should never take these off," she said. They slipped them around their necks.

"And you should never, ever, play near the MoleTroll hole again," Pa added.

Toby looked at Trixie. "I promise."

Trixie nodded. "I don't want to see a MoleTroll again as long as I live."

Tabby, seeing that there wasn't any string tied to her belt, and thinking that she still had wings, tried to fly away. But she just jumped and fell.

"Looking for these?" Toby smiled, holding out her wings.

"She's not a baby anymore," their mother said regretfully.

"I think we ought to go home now," Pa Troll said. "I'd like to write this story down."

*   *   *

43

When the second cover was placed on top of the old one, the torch was left burning beside it to remind Trolls of the danger below.

But even with two covers, when the evening wind is calm and the night is silent, you can hear the MoleTrolls scratching to get out.

*   *   *

We hope you enjoyed our first
Troll Family Adventure.

Join us next time for

Lost in L.A.

When a hot air balloon lands in the Troll's forest,
the three little trolls end up lost in Los Angeles.
It's a non-stop adventure as they
try to find their way back home.